Kate Greenaway
1888

하멜른의
피리 부는 사나이

시

로버트 브라우닝

삽화 35장

케이트 그리너웨이

목판제작

에드먼드 에반스

번역

이한이

클라시코 레트로북

도서출판 소와다리
COW & BRIDGE PUBLISHING Co.

서울, 런던, 뉴욕, 도쿄

Printed in the Republic of Korea.
Graphite Engine™ remastered by Edward Graphic Centre.
Korean translation 2017 © Sowadari Publishing Co. 2017 all rights reserved.

FIRST PRINTING

하멜른의 피리 부는 사나이

I.

이름난 도시 하노버 가까운 곳,
브라운슈바이크에 하멜른 마을 있다네.
깊고 넓은 베저강,
남쪽 성벽 휘감아 흐르는,
예보다 아늑한 곳 본 적이 없다네.
하지만 이 노래 시작되는,
한 오백 년 전만 해도,
들짐승에 시달리는 마을 사람들,
딱해 눈뜨고 볼 수가 없었네.

II.

쥐새끼들!

개와 싸우고 고양이를 죽이고,

요람에 잠이 든 아기를 깨물고,

치즈 통에 들어 있는 치즈를 갉아 먹고,

국자에 묻어 있는 국물을 핥아 먹고,

소금에 절여 놓은 생선 통을 뒤엎고,
남정네들 나들이 모자 속에 새끼 치고,

아낙네들 조잘대는 수다마저 훼방 놨네,

Kate Greenaway

목소리까지 집어삼키는,
쩍쩍 소리 끽끽 소리로,
오십 가지 각기 다른 높고 낮은 소리로.

III.

급기야 마을 사람들,
회관으로 몰려와,
소리쳤네 "얼간이 같은 시장 놈아!"
"의원들도 똑같아— 세상에,"

Kate Greenaway

"담비 털 의원복을 거저 입혀 주다니."
"쥐새끼들 어떻게 쫓아낼지,"
"생각도 못 하고 안 하는 멍청이들에게!"
"피둥피둥 늙어도 모피 옷만 두르면,"
"빈둥빈둥 놀아도 될 줄 알았지?"
"정신 차려 이 양반들아 머리를 굴리라고!"
"굶어 죽기 전에 해결책을 찾으라고!"
"안 그러면 쫓겨날 줄 알라고!"
시장나리 의원나리 이 말 듣고,
깜짝 놀라 벌벌 떠네.

IV.

회의 시작 한 시간 만,
시장 마침내 침묵을 깼네.
"단돈 한 냥에 이 옷을 팔고 싶구먼."
"차라리 옆 마을에 살았더라면!"
"돌아가며 하나씩 묘안을 짜냅시다——,"
"불쌍한 내 머리 다시 지끈거리오."
"내 아무리 쥐어짜도 말짱 헛일이었소."
"오 그렇지, 덫, 덫, 덫!"
바로 그 순간 나는 소리 다름 아닌 노크 소리,
회의실 문가에서 조심스레 "똑, 똑, 똑!"
"깜짝이야!" 시장이 소리친다, "무슨 소리지?"
시장은 의원들과 함께 앉아 있었네.
몸집은 땅딸하고 살집은 똥똥했네.
까 놓은 지 한참 지난 굴보다도,
메마른 칙칙한 눈은,
초록빛 걸쭉한 거북이 수프 달라고,
똥배가 요동치는 점심때만 반짝였네.
"바닥에 신발 터는 소리인가, 툭툭툭?"
"찍찍찍, 쥐새끼 비슷한 소리만 들려도,"
"가슴 뛰네 팔딱팔딱!"

V.

"들어오시게!"── 거만하게 시장이 외치자,
들어왔네 희한한 자!
머리부터 발끝까지 걸친 긴 외투는,
요상도 하여라 반은 노랑 반은 빨강,
큰 키에 깡마른 사내,
새파란 눈동자 바늘처럼 째진 눈,
풀어 헤친 담색 머리 살결은 거무데데,
털 없는 구레나룻 수염 없는 턱,
미소를 지을 듯 말 듯 실룩이는 입술,
어디 사는 누구인지 짐작조차 가지 않는,
기묘한 차림새 키 큰 사내,
혀를 차지 않을 이 누구 있으랴.
한 의원이 속닥이길 "보아하니 우리 증조부 영감이구먼."
"지옥 나팔소리에 무덤에서 걸어 나온 게야!"
"묘비를 저렇게 칠했었지!"

VI.

그 사내 탁자 앞에 다가와,
"존경하는 나리님들," 하고 "저로 말할 것 같으면,"
"신비한 마법으로,"
"하늘 아래 살아 있는,"
"날고 뛰고 기고 헤엄치는 모든 짐승 꾀어내어,"
"끌고 갈 수 있습지요, 다시는 눈에 띄지 않게!"
"마법은 주로,"
"두더지, 도롱뇽, 두꺼비, 살무사,"
"사람에게 해 끼치는 짐승에게 겁니다요."
"사람들을 저를 이리 부릅지요."
"얼룩빼기 피리쟁이."
의원들 그제야 눈길 주네 사내 목 언저리에.
노랑 빨강 외투와 어울리는,
노랑 빨강 줄무늬 목도리에.

목도리 끝에 매달린 피리에.
불고 싶어 안달이 났는지,
낡아 빠진 옷자락 위로,
늘어뜨린 피리 위에서,
꿈지럭대는 손가락에.

"소인 비록," 사내 입을 여네 "미천한 피리쟁이."
"허나 지난 유월 어마어마한 모기떼로부터,"
"타타르[1] 황제를 구했습죠."
"무시무시한 흡혈박쥐 떼로부터,"
"인도 왕도 구했습죠."
"그리고 나리님들 골칫거리 말씀인데,"
"이 마을에서 쥐를 쫓아드리면,"
"천 냥을 주시겠습니까?"
"천 냥? 오만 냥 줌세!" —— 의원과 시장 놀라,
그렇게 외쳤다네.

1) **타타르** : 동부 유럽에서 서부 아시아 일대 옛 몽골의 대제국

VII.

거리로 나섰네 피리 부는 사나이,
옅은 미소 지으며.
그는 알지 조용한 피리 속에,
어떤 마법 잠자는지.
이윽고 솜씨 좋은 음악가처럼,
피리를 불기 위해 입술을 오므렸네.
쪽 째진 눈에서는 녹색 푸른색 불꽃이 번쩍.
소금 뿌린 촛불 같네.
그리고 삐리리 세 음 불기 무섭게,
발걸음 소리 희미하게 들려오고,

발걸음 소리 쿵쿵 소리 되고,
쿵쿵 소리에 우르릉 땅이 울리더니,
쥐들이 집 밖으로 나오네 재주를 넘으며.
큰 쥐, 작은 쥐, 호리호리한 쥐, 통통한 쥐,
갈색 쥐, 검은색 쥐, 회색 쥐, 노란색 쥐,
점잖은 늙은 쥐, 촐싹대는 어린 쥐,

아빠 쥐, 엄마 쥐, 삼촌 쥐, 조카 쥐,
꼬리 치켜 올린 쥐, 수염 쫑긋 세운 쥐,
수십 마리 가족 쥐,
형제 쥐, 자매 쥐, 남편 쥐, 아내 쥐,
피리쟁이를 뒤따르네 필사적으로.
피리쟁이 나아가네, 이 골목 저 골목으로.
쥐들은 춤추며 따르네, 발에 발맞추어.
베저강에 이르러서,
모두 뛰어들어 죽을 때까지!
── 살아남은 딱 한 마리, 줄리어스 시저처럼 굳센 쥐.
헤엄쳐 강을 건너 고향인 쥐 왕국에,
이 소식 전했네.
(그리고 글로 적어 소중히 간직했네.)
소식인즉 "피리 첫 음이,"
"곱창 손질하는 소리로 들렸고,"
"잘 익은 사과에서,"
"즙 짜내는 소리,"
"절인 채소 통 따는 소리,"
"과일 상자 여는 소리,"
"고래기름 통 마개 뽑는 소리,"
"버터 통 뚜껑 따는 소리,"
"그건 마치 목소리 같았네."
(하프며 가야금 소리보다 훨씬 감미로운 울림으로,)
"오 쥐들아 기뻐하렴!"
"이 세상은 거대한 어물전이 되었단다!"
"아삭아삭 갉으렴, 오독오독 씹으렴, 간식을 먹으렴."
"아침도 점심도 저녁도 실컷 먹으렴!"
"커다란 설탕 통은 이미 부서져,"
"거대한 태양처럼 눈부시게 빛났네."
"그것도 내 코앞에서."
"마치 이렇게 말하는 듯했네, 와서 나를 밀치고 가렴!"
"── 아차, 베저강이 내 머리 위에 있더군."

Kate Greenaway

VIII.

들리는가 교회당 다 떠나가도록,
하멜른 사람들 종 치는 소리가.
"가서," 시장이 소리치길 "기다란 장대를 가져다가,"
"쑤셔라 쥐구멍 막아라 쥐구멍!"

"목수와 미장이에게 일러라."
"우리 마을에 쥐새끼 발자국조차,"
"남기지 말라고!"── 장터에 있던,
피리쟁이 고개를 들고 불쑥,
말하기를 "이제 천 냥을 주시지요!"

IX.

천 냥! 새파랗게 질린 시장,
의원들도 마찬가지.
보르도 적포도주, 모젤 백포도주, 그라브 포도주, 라인 포도주는,
의회 만찬으로 동이 났지.
그 돈 반만 있어도 지하 창고 제일 큰 술통을,
라인 백포도주로 가득 채울 텐데.
전부 주어야만 하는가,
노랑 빨강 외투 걸친 떠돌이 집시에게!
의원들에게 눈짓하며 시장은 말했네 "그게 말이네,"
"우리 거래는 강가에서 끝났네."
"쥐새끼들 빠지는 걸 두 눈으로 봤다네."
"한번 죽은 건 되살아날 수 없다네."
"자네에게 한잔 대접할 의무를 마다할,"
"친구, 우린 그런 사람 아닐세."
"자네 주머니에 찔러 줄 돈도 그렇고."
"돈 얘기가 나왔으니, 우리가 했던 말은,"
"몇 냥이었더라, 자네도 잘 알다시피, 농담이었네."
"그게 말이네, 우리도 손해가 막심해 아껴야 하네."
"천 냥? 오십 냥! 자 받게."

X.

마음 상한 피리쟁이 소리치길,
"장난일랑 마시오! 나는 더 기다릴 수가 없소."
"약속했다오, 저녁 만찬 때까지 바그다드에 가기로."
"대접한다오, 칼리프1)의 요리사가 진귀한 음식을."
"보답이라오, 부엌에 득실대는 전갈을 몰아내 준."
"그가 증명하오, 이 몸 싸구려 몰이꾼이 아님을."
"그대 명심하오, 이 몸 푼돈에 물러나지 않음을!"
"나를 노하게 한 그대들,"
"보게 될 것이오, 피리 부는 내 뒤를 따르는 무리를."

XI.

"무어라?" 시장이 호통치네 "내가 참을 것 같나?"
"하찮은 요리사보다 내가 못하다는 말을."
"나를 모욕하다니 엉터리 피리 들고 색동 누더기 걸친,"
"천박한 잡놈 주제에."
"우리를 협박했겠다? 친구 멋대로 해 보시지."
"어디 한번 불어 보시지 입술 부르틀 때까지!"

---

1) **칼리프** : 정치와 종교의 권력을 아울러 갖는 이슬람 교단의 지배자

XII.

또다시 거리로 나섰네 피리 부는 사나이.
다시 한 번 입술이,
곧고 매끄러운 기다란 피리 물고,

삐리리 세 음 불기도 전에,

지금껏 어떤 음악가도 흉내 낼 수 없었던,
너무나 부드럽고 매혹적인 음계 울려 퍼지네.

와당탕쿵탕

야단법석이라도 났는지.

아이들 흥에 겨워 밀치락달치락,

작은 발 아장아장 나막신 달가닥달가닥,

고사리손 짝짝짝 앵두 입술 조잘조잘,

모이 뿌린 마당에 닭 달려들듯,

뛰어나오는 아이들.

사내아이 계집아이 하나같이,

장밋빛 붉은 볼 황금빛 곱슬머리,

반짝이는 눈동자 진주알 같은 이,

사뿐사뿐

폴짝폴짝

홍겹게

소리치며 깔깔대며 황홀한 음악 소리 따라가네.

XIII.

시장은 입이 붙고 의원들 발이 붙었네.
마치 나무토막으로 변해 버린 양,
한 발짝도 한 마디도 떼지 못한 채,
아이들 흥겨이 폴짝폴짝 지나가는데,

—— 눈 뜨고 지켜만 보았네,
피리쟁이 뒤따르는 즐거운 아이들을.
얼마나 괴로웠을까 시장의 마음은,
얼마나 두근댔을까 의원들의 가슴은.
피리쟁이 큰길가에서,
마을의 아들딸을 데리고,
소용돌이치는 베저강으로 돌아들 적에!
하지만 피리쟁이 발걸음 돌리네,
남에서 서로 코펠베르크 산으로.
피리 부는 사나이 따라 몰려가는,
아이들 가슴속에 기쁨이 넘치네.
"드높은 산봉우리를 넘을 수는 없겠지."
"힘들어 피리를 떨구게 되겠지."
"그러면 아이들도 걸음을 멈추겠지."
아! 아이들이 산비탈에 다다르자,
신비한 문 활짝 열리네,
동굴이라도 갑자기 뚫린 것처럼.
피리쟁이 앞장서니 아이들 뒤따르네.
마지막 한 아이까지 모두 들어가자,
산비탈 문 순식간에 닫히네.
모두라고 했나? 아니! 절름발이 한 아이만,
춤추며 따라가지 못했네.
여러 해 지나고 그 아이 슬퍼함을 꾸짖으니,
이렇게 대꾸했네——.
"우리 마을은 따분해요, 친구들 떠난 후로!"
"잊을 수가 없어요, 나만 빼고,"
"친구들이 보게 될 멋진 광경을."
"피리 부는 아저씨가 데려다 준다고,"
"나에게도 약속했던 행복한 나라에,"
"이제 거의 다 왔다고."

Kate Greenaway

"맑은 물 샘솟고 과일나무 자라는 곳."
"꽃들은 더 어여쁜 빛깔로 피어나고,"
"온통 처음 보는 신기한 것들."
"우리 마을 공작새보다 참새가 더 화려하고,"
"우리 마을 꽃사슴보다 강아지가 더 빠르고,"
"꿀벌은 독침이 없고,"
"독수리 날개 달린 말이 태어난다던 곳."
"그래서 나는 믿었죠,"
"내 다리도 곧 나으리라."
"하지만 음악 소리 그치고 나는 서 있었죠."
"혼자만 덩그러니,"
"언덕에 남았죠, 그토록 바랐건만."
"나는 절뚝대요, 여전히."
"그 나라 이야기는 들을 수 없었죠, 다시는!"

XIV.

아아, 가엾어라 하멜른이여!
많은 사람들 마음에,
부자가 천국 문으로 들어가는 것보다,
낙타가 바늘귀로 들어가는 것이 쉽다는,
성경 말씀 새겨졌네.
시장은 소문을 퍼뜨렸네.
입에서 입으로 동에서 서로 남에서 북으로,
피리쟁이 있을 만한 곳이라면 어디고.
금과 은을 주겠노라 그대 마음 흡족할 만큼.
떠나간 길 되돌아오기만 한다면.
따라간 아이들 데리고만 온다면.
하지만 깨달았네, 가망 없는 헛된 노력임을.
피리쟁이와 춤추던 아이들 가 버렸네 영원히.
시장과 의원들 법을 만들었네, 관리들은,

Kate Greenaway

문서에 날짜를 절차대로 적어야 한다는.
예를 들어 몇 년 몇 월 며칠 뒤에는,
이 글귀를 빠뜨려서는 아니 된다는.
"1376년 7월 22일"
"그 일이 있은 후로,"
"세월이 얼마얼마 흘렀다."
그리고 더욱더 단단히 기억하고자,
아이들이 마지막으로 지나간 길,
이렇게 이름 붙였네.
"피리 부는 사나이의 거리."
피리를 불거나 북을 치면 아이 잃게 되는 길.
여관이나 식당에서 떠드는 이 없었고,
엄숙한 거리에서 웃는 이 없었네.
하지만 동굴이 생겼던 맞은편에,
비석 세워 이 이야기 새겼네.
또한 세상에 알리고자,
어떻게 아이들을 빼앗겨 버렸는지,
커다란 교회 창에 이 이야기 그렸고,
지금도 그 자리에 남아 있다네.
그리고 빠뜨려선 안 될 이야기.
트란실바니아[1] 어느 마을에,
이국 풍습 낯선 차림의,
이방인들 살고 있다네.
이웃 마을 사람들 하는 이야기.
그들의 조상은 아주 오래전에,
한꺼번에 모조리 유괴되어,
지하 감옥에 갇혀 있다가,
빠져나온 사람들.
어쩌 된 일인지 영문은 모르지만,
고향은 브라운슈바이크 하멜른 마을이라네.

1) 트란실바니아 : 루마니아 북서부 지방

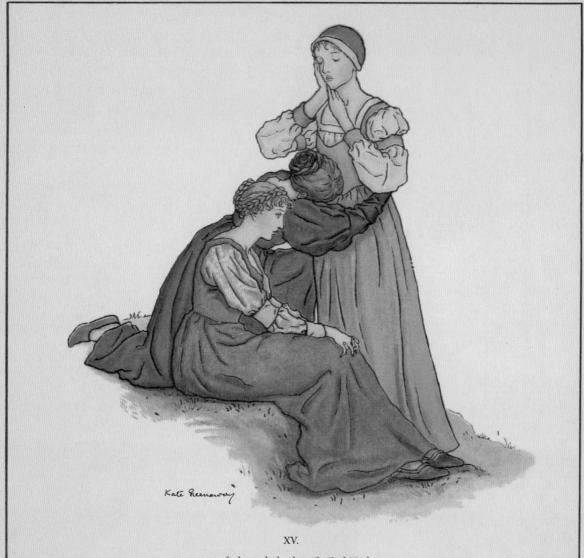

XV.

그러니 꼬마야 위로해 주자꾸나.
모든 이의 아픔을── 특히 피리쟁이를!
그리고 새앙쥐든 시궁쥐든,
피리 불어 쫓아 주거든,
약속한 것 무엇이든,
지키도록 하자꾸나!

The
Pied Piper
of
Hamelin

THE PIED PIPER

OF

HAMELIN

BY

ROBERT BROWNING

WITH 35 ILLUSTRATIONS

BY

KATE GREENAWAY

ENGRAVED AND PRINTED IN COLOURS BY EDMUND EVANS

LONDON

GEORGE ROUTLEDGE AND SONS

BROADWAY, LUDGATE HILL

GLASGOW AND NEW YORK

The Pied Piper of Hamelin.

I.

HAMELIN Town's in Brunswick,
By famous Hanover city;
The river Weser, deep and wide,
Washes its wall on the southern side;
A pleasanter spot you never spied;
But, when begins my ditty,
Almost five hundred years ago,
To see the townsfolk suffer so
From vermin, was a pity.

II.

Rats!
They fought the dogs and killed the cats,
And bit the babies in the cradles,
And ate the cheeses out of the vats,
And licked the soup from the cooks'
own ladles,

The Pied Piper of Hamelin

Split open the kegs of salted sprats,
Made nests inside men's Sunday hats,
And even spoiled the women's chats,
    By drowning their speaking
    With shrieking and squeaking
In fifty different sharps and flats.

III.

At last the people in a body
    To the Town Hall came flocking:
"'Tis clear," cried they, "our Mayor's a noddy;
    "And as for our Corporation—shocking
"To think we buy gowns lined with ermine
"For dolts that can't or won't determine
"What's best to rid us of our vermin!
"You hope, because you're old and obese,
"To find in the furry civic robe ease?
"Rouse up, sirs! Give your brains a racking
"To find the remedy we're lacking,
"Or, sure as fate, we'll send you packing!"
At this the Mayor and Corporation
Quaked with a mighty consternation.

IV.

An hour they sate in council,

 At length the Mayor broke silence:

"For a guilder I'd my ermine gown sell;

 "I wish I were a mile hence!

"It's easy to bid one rack one's brain—

"I'm sure my poor head aches again,

"I've scratched it so, and all in vain

"Oh for a trap, a trap, a trap!"

Just as he said this, what should hap

At the chamber door but a gentle tap?

"Bless us," cried the Mayor, "what's that?"

(With the Corporation as he sat,

Looking little though wondrous fat;

Nor brighter was his eye, nor moister

Than a too-long-opened oyster,

Save when at noon his paunch grew mutinous

For a plate of turtle green and glutinous)

"Only a scraping of shoes on the mat?

"Anything like the sound of a rat

"Makes my heart go pit-a-pat!"

The Pied Piper of Hamelin

V.

"Come in!"—the Mayor cried, looking bigger:
And in did come the strangest figure!
His queer long coat from heel to head
Was half of yellow and half of red,
And he himself was tall and thin,
With sharp blue eyes, each like a pin,
And light loose hair, yet swarthy skin
No tuft on cheek nor beard on chin,
But lips where smile went out and in;
There was no guessing his kith and kin:
And nobody could enough admire
The tall man and his quaint attire.
Quoth one: "It's as my great-grandsire,
"Starting up at the Trump of Doom's tone,
"Had walked this way from his painted tombstone!"

VI.

He advanced to the council-table:
And, "Please your honours," said he, "I'm able,
"By means of a secret charm, to draw
"All creatures living beneath the sun,
"That creep or swim or fly or run,
"After me so as you never saw!

The Pied Piper of Hamelin

"And I chiefly use my charm
"On creatures that do people harm,
"The mole and toad and newt and viper;
"And people call me the Pied Piper."
(And here they noticed round his neck
A scarf of red and yellow stripe,
To match with his coat of the self-same cheque;
And at the scarf's end hung a pipe;
And his fingers, they noticed, were ever straying
As if impatient to be playing
Upon this pipe, as low it dangled
Over his vesture so old-fangled.)
"Yet," said he, "poor piper as I am,
"In Tartary I freed the Cham,
"Last June, from his huge swarms of gnats,
"I eased in Asia the Nizam
"Of a monstrous brood of vampyre-bats:
"And as for what your brain bewilders,
"If I can rid your town of rats
"Will you give me a thousand guilders?"
"One? fifty thousand!"—was the exclamation
Of the astonished Mayor and Corporation.

VII.

Into the street the Piper stept,
    Smiling first a little smile,
As if he knew what magic slept
    In his quiet pipe the while;
Then, like a musical adept,
To blow the pipe his lips he wrinkled,
And green and blue his sharp eyes twinkled,
Like a candle-flame where salt is sprinkled;
And ere three shrill notes the pipe uttered,
You heard as if an army muttered;
And the muttering grew to a grumbling;
And the grumbling grew to a mighty rumbling;
And out of the houses the rats came tumbling.
Great rats, small rats, lean rats, brawny rats,
Brown rats, black rats, grey rats, tawny rats,
Grave old plodders, gay young friskers,
    Fathers, mothers, uncles, cousins,
Cocking tails and pricking whiskers,
    Families by tens and dozens,
Brothers, sisters, husbands, wives—
Followed the Piper for their lives.

The Pied Piper of Hamelin

From street to street he piped advancing,
And step for step they followed dancing,
Until they came to the river Weser
Wherein all plunged and perished!
— Save one who, stout as Julius Caesar,
Swam across and lived to carry
(As he, the manuscript he cherished)
To Rat-land home his commentary:
Which was, "At the first shrill notes of the
          pipe,
"I heard a sound as of scraping tripe,
"And putting apples, wondrous ripe,
"Into a cider-press's gripe:
"And a moving away of pickle-tub-boards,
"And a leaving ajar of conserve-cupboards,
"And a drawing the corks of train-oil-flasks,
"And a breaking the hoops of butter-casks:
"And it seemed as if a voice
"(Sweeter far than by harp or by psaltery
"Is breathed) called out, 'Oh rats, rejoice!
"'The world is grown to one vast drysaltery!
"'So munch on, crunch on, take your nuncheon,
"'Breakfast, supper, dinner, luncheon!'

"And just as a bulky sugar-puncheon,
"All ready staved, like a great sun shone
"Glorious scarce an inch before me,
"Just as methought it said, 'Come, bore me!'
"—I found the Weser rolling o'er me."

VIII.

You should have heard the Hamelin people
Ringing the bells till they rocked the steeple
"Go," cried the Mayor, "and get long poles,
"Poke out the nests and block up the holes!
"Consult with carpenters and builders,
"And leave in our town not even a trace
"Of the rats!"—when suddenly, up the face
Of the Piper perked in the market-place,
With a, "First, if you please, my thousand
        guilders!"

IX.

A thousand guilders! The Mayor looked blue;
So did the Corporation too.
For council dinners made rare havoc
With Claret, Moselle, Vin-de-Grave, Hock;

And half the money would replenish
Their cellar's biggest butt with Rhenish.
To pay this sum to a wandering fellow
With a gipsy coat of red and yellow!
"Beside," quoth the Mayor with a knowing wink,
"Our business was done at the river's brink;
"We saw with our eyes the vermin sink,
"And what's dead can't come to life, I think.
"So, friend, we're not the folks to shrink
"From the duty of giving you something to drink,
"And a matter of money to put in your poke;
"But as for the guilders, what we spoke
"Of them, as you very well know, was in joke.
"Beside, our losses have made us thrifty.
"A thousand guilders! Come, take fifty!"

X.

The Piper's face fell, and he cried,
"No trifling! I can't wait, beside!
"I've promised to visit by dinner-time
"Bagdad, and accept the prime
"Of the Head-Cook's pottage, all he's rich in,
"For having left, in the Caliph's kitchen,

"Of a nest of scorpions no survivor:
"With him I proved no bargain-driver,
"With you, don't think I'll bate a stiver!
"And folks who put me in a passion
"May find me pipe after another fashion."

XI.

"How?" cried the Mayor, "d'ye think I brook
"Being worse treated than a Cook?
"Insulted by a lazy ribald
"With idle pipe and vesture piebald?
"You threaten us, fellow? Do your worst,
"Blow your pipe there till you burst!"

XII.

Once more he stept into the street,
    And to his lips again
Laid his long pipe of smooth straight cane;
    And ere he blew three notes (such sweet
Soft notes as yet musician's cunning
    Never gave the enraptured air)
There was a rustling that seemed like a bustling
Of merry crowds justling at pitching and hustling,

Small feet were pattering, wooden shoes clattering,
Little hands clapping and little tongues chattering,
And, like fowls in a farm-yard when barley is
      scattering,
Out came the children running.
All the little boys and girls,
With rosy cheeks and flaxen curls,
And sparkling eyes and teeth like pearls,
Tripping and skipping, ran merrily after
The wonderful music with shouting and laughter.

XIII.

The Mayor was dumb, and the Council stood
As if they were changed into blocks of wood,
Unable to move a step, or cry
To the children merrily skipping by,
— Could only follow with the eye
That joyous crowd at the Piper's back.
But how the Mayor was on the rack,
And the wretched Council's bosoms beat,
As the Piper turned from the High Street
To where the Weser rolled its waters
Right in the way of their sons and daughters!

However he turned from South to West,

And to Koppelberg Hill his steps addressed,

And after him the children pressed;

Great was the joy in every breast.

"He never can cross that mighty top!

"He's forced to let the piping drop,

"And we shall see our children stop!"

When, lo, as they reached the mountain-side,

A wondrous portal opened wide,

As if a cavern was suddenly hollowed;

And the Piper advanced and the children followed,

And when all were in to the very last,

The door in the mountain-side shut fast.

Did I say, all? No! One was lame,

And could not dance the whole of the way;

And in after years, if you would blame

His sadness, he was used to say,—

"It's dull in our town since my playmates left!

"I can't forget that I'm bereft

"Of all the pleasant sights they see,

"Which the Piper also promised me.

"For he led us, he said, to a joyous land,

"Joining the town and just at hand,

The Pied Piper of Hamelin

"Where waters gushed and fruit-trees grew,

"And flowers put forth a fairer hue,

"And everything was strange and new;

"The sparrows were brighter than peacocks here,

"And their dogs outran our fallow deer,

"And honey-bees had lost their stings,

"And horses were born with eagles' wings;

"And just as I became assured

"My lame foot would be speedily cured,

"The music stopped and I stood still,

"And found myself outside the hill,

"Left alone against my will,

"To go now limping as before,

"And never hear of that country more!"

XIV.

Alas, alas for Hamelin!

　　There came into many a burgher's pate

　　A text which says that heaven's gate

　　Opes to the rich at as easy rate

As the needle's eye takes a camel in!

The mayor sent East, West, North and South,

To offer the Piper, by word of mouth,

The Pied Piper of Hamelin

Wherever it was men's lot to find him,
Silver and gold to his heart's content,
If he'd only return the way he went,
    And bring the children behind him.
But when they saw 'twas a lost endeavour,
And Piper and dancers were gone for ever,
They made a decree that lawyers never
    Should think their records dated duly
If, after the day of the month and year,
These words did not as well appear,
"And so long after what happened here
    "On the Twenty-second of July,
"Thirteen hundred and seventy-six:"
And the better in memory to fix
The place of the children's last retreat,
They called it, the Pied Piper's Street—
Where any one playing on pipe or tabor,
Was sure for the future to lose his labour.
Nor suffered they hostelry or tavern
    To shock with mirth a street so solemn;
But opposite the place of the cavern
    They wrote the story on a column,
And on the great church-window painted

The Pied Piper of Hamelin

The same, to make the world acquainted
How their children were stolen away,
And there it stands to this very day.
And I must not omit to say
That in Transylvania there's a tribe
Of alien people who ascribe
The outlandish ways and dress
On which their neighbours lay such stress,
To their fathers and mothers having risen
Out of some subterraneous prison
Into which they were trepanned
Long time ago in a mighty band
Out of Hamelin town in Brunswick land,
But how or why, they don't understand.

XV.

So, Willy, let me and you be wipers
Of scores out with all men — especially pipers!
And, whether they pipe us free from rats or
    from mice,
If we've promised them aught, let us keep
    our promise!

First published 1888
Original wood block designs engraved
by Edmund Evans

CLASSICO

Part of Cow & Bridge Publishing Co.

Web site : www.cafe.naver.com/sowadari

3ga-302, 6-21, 40th St., Guwolro, Namgu, Incheon, #402-848 South Korea

Telephone 0505-719-7787 Facsimile 0505-719-7788 Email sowadari@naver.com

"The Pied Piper of Hamelin"

Original poem written by Robert Browning

First original edition published by George Routledge and Sons, Glasgow & New York

Illustrations by Kate Greenaway and Engraved by Edmund Evans

This recovering edition published by Cow & Bridge Publishing Co. Korea

2017 © Cow & Bridge Publishing Co. all rights reserved.

하멜른의 피리 부는 사나이

지은이 로버트 브라우닝 │ **옮긴이** 이한이

원화 케이트 그리너웨이 │ **목판** 에드먼드 에반스 │ **디자인** 김동근

1판 1쇄 2017년 6월 25일 │ **발행인** 김동근 │ **발행처** 도서출판 소와다리

주소 인천시 남구 구월로 40번길 6-21 제302호

대표전화 0505-719-7787 │ **팩스** 0505-719-7788 │ **이메일** sowadari@naver.com

ISBN 978-89-98046-80-4 (04840)